Promises and Kisses From a Boss

Nikki Rae

Tyanna Presents

Synopsis

Twenty-three-year-old Lacey Daye has dreamed about marrying Kendrick Mason ever since she was in middle school. Lacey thought that once she and Kendrick got together, everything would be a walk in the park. She couldn't have been more wrong. It's no secret that Kendrick loves Lacey, but he loves the streets just as much. Pregnant and with their marriage on the horizon, Lacey pressures Kendrick to leave the game, causing chaos on the home front. He feels stuck between a rock and a hard place

Caught up in the drama, neither one of them wants to compromise. Will all the arguing that Kendrick and Lacey do pull them apart and push him further into the streets? Or, will the love that Kendrick and Lacey share be enough to keep their relationship on a straight path and lead them to the altar to live happily ever after? Find out as we take a rollercoaster ride in this drama-filled Valentine's

Day novella...

Lacey

I was sitting in the doctor's office waiting to be called to the back, and Kendrick still hadn't got here yet. I just prayed that he didn't miss our first appointment.

"Lacey Daye?" the nurse called me back.

I got up and looked around to see if Kendrick was walking through the door, but he wasn't. I had just found out that I was pregnant two weeks ago and was here for my first prenatal care appointment. I just know he bet not miss this appointment, or it will be hell to pay. After the nurse took my weight and blood pressure, the door opened, and in walked Kendrick. He walked over and kissed my lips.

"Hey, baby. I'm sorry I'm late. I swear, I'll make it up to you," he said.

I hated that I couldn't stay mad at Kendrick for long. The doctor came in and did an exam and told me that I just eight weeks today, which meant I had a long way to go. She gave me my script for prenatal vitamins and an appointment for two months from now. When we left the doctor's office, Kendrick wanted to grab something to eat. We decided to eat at Bob Evans, and Kendrick walked me to my car before going to his car.

My name is Lacey Daye, and I'm the youngest of two. I have a brother who's two years older than I am. I'm twenty-three, and he's twenty-five. The two of us are extremely close. Although we are only two years apart, Liam was the one who always made sure I was straight. My parents were still around and still together, but they were too busy drinking to remember that they had two kids. So we had to fend for ourselves, but I have no complaints because we were doing pretty well for ourselves. My brother and I were born and raised in Camden, New Jersey.

Kendrick and I have been together for almost two years. It would be two years on Valentine's Day, which was just five months away. Valentine's Day was also our upcoming wedding day. Kendrick was a boss in the streets of Camden, and he had money for days, so when we got together, he made sure I was good. He helped me get my first apartment and first car. He also just bought me my hair and spa salon. I haven't opened the shop up yet because we were in a Covid-19 Pandemic, so I had to be careful about how I moved, especially while being pregnant. I was still having some work done to the shop, so when I did decide to open it, everything would be perfect.

I've known Kendrick since I was in the eighth grade. Kendrick is my best friend's brother. Kendra, my best friend, and I have been best friends since the eighth grade. And from the day I laid eyes on Kendrick, I was in love, but he was too old for me at the time. I was only thirteen, and he was eighteen. No matter how drunk my parents got, they would have made sure he went to jail if they even thought that he was thinking about messing with me. I was too shy to ever tell Kendrick that I liked him, but Kendra had already made it clear that he would never talk to me while I was a minor and that she wasn't sure if he would want to mess with me when I turned of age. Hell, I didn't think that he would mess with me, either. I saw him mess around with so many women, but he never claimed any of them as his girl.

As soon as we walked into Bob Evans, we were seated right away, and I was glad because I was too hungry to wait. Plus, I couldn't wait to get home so I could take this stupid ass mask off. I hated walking around with a mask on.

"Kendrick, why were you late to the appointment?" I asked as soon as we finished ordering our food.

"I got caught up with some shit, and I had to take care of it ASAP."

"You had shit to do that was more important than our child?"

"Look, don't start, Lacey. You know nothing is more important than you or my baby. I didn't even miss anything. You just bitching just because."

I hated when me and Kendrick got into arguments or went back forth with one another because it could get pretty bad between the two of us. And most of the time, after it's all said and done, we don't really be arguing over shit that doesn't even be worth the fight. I didn't bother to say anything because I wasn't in the mood to argue with him right now.

"Whatever, Kendrick. I don't feel like arguing about this."

After we finished eating, he claimed he had to handle some business, so I decided to link up with Kendra.

I pulled up to Kendra's apartment and knocked on the door. A few moments later, she opened up the door and let me in.

"Hey, best friend. How did the visit go?"

"The visit was okay. Of course, your brother was late, talking about, he had something to take care of. I'm so over this street shit with him," I told her.

"Lacey, you know you my homegirl, and I love you, but you cannot act like you didn't know what you were getting into when you started fucking with Kendrick. You knew him for quite some time before fucking with him. I love Kendrick, but he's a piece of work."

I knew what Kendra was saying was true. That was the thing about Kendra. She didn't hold her tongue for anyone. Kendrick was a piece of work, but I loved him so much. When Kendrick and I weren't going back and forth, we're great with one another.

After chilling with Kindra a little longer, I decided to go home and take a nap. On the way home, I decided to call Kendrick, but as usual, he didn't answer the phone. When I got in the house, I went into my room and laid across the bed. Before I knew it, I had dozed off.

Kendrick

"Shit, Sharee, suck this dick." I groaned through gritted teeth as I guided her head up and down on my thickness.

Sharee was a chick that I fucked with from time to time when I needed to relieve some stress. We haven't fucked in a minute, but every now and then, I'd let her give me head. Sharee can suck the hell out of some dick. I swear, when it came to deep throating, she was the only chick that could handle all the dick that I was packing. After busting in Sharee's mouth, I contemplated if I wanted to fuck or not, but I decided against it. I needed to get home to Lacey.

The name is Kendrick Mason, and I'm twenty-eight years old. I was born and raised in Camden, New Jersey. I came from a two-parent home, and both of my parents were successful in their careers, but I have always been into fast money. So I started selling drugs at the age of fourteen, and now I'm a boss in the streets. I had the best dope and weed in the hood. I had more money than I knew what to do with. Although I loved money, I loved saving it even more. I had my own shit, but I wasn't all extra with mine. I had a nice house and two cars, and that's all I needed it.

Niggas be doing dumb shit with their money trying to floss, but I was the complete opposite of the average hustler. Now that Lacey was pregnant with my first seed, I was starting to move a little differently. I planned to be out of the game before Lacey and I got married and before my seed was born. I haven't told Lacey yet. She hasn't given me a chance because lately, all she did was bitch and complain about everything. I wasn't the type of nigga that was going to argue back and forth, especially over dumb shit.

I loved Lacey with everything in me and would never put another woman before her. I fucked around on her from time to time, but those other women didn't mean shit to me. They were just something to do when I was bored or pissed with Lacey. I knew what I was doing wasn't cool, but I was working on it. What I did know was, after we tied the knot, Lacey would be my one and only. No matter what happened between me and Lacey, I couldn't picture life without her. Although Valentine's Day and our upcoming wedding day would be two years since we've been together, we were dating for about six months before that.

Lacey was a good girl, and I will always love and respect her. Lacey wasn't a fast ass like the rest of these girls. She wanted to make sure she had something going for herself so she didn't have to depend on anyone. She wasn't hot in the ass, and she was loyal and honest. Lacey was my sister's best friend, but they were complete opposites. I wished that Kendra was more like Lacey if I could be honest. My sister was a fast ass and was one of these chicks that believed in a man taking care of her, so she didn't work.

I pulled up to Lacey's apartment and used my key. When I walked in, Lacey wasn't in the living room, so I went to the bedroom, and she was on the bed knocked out. I wanted Lacey to move in with me, but she said that she didn't want us to live together until we were married. I couldn't do anything but respect that. Even though we didn't live together, we spent most nights together, so it felt like we lived together anyway. I walked into the bathroom and washed off before going back into the bedroom. I watched Lacey sleep for about two minutes before I decided to pull her pants down and wake her up with some mind-blowing head. When Lacey opened her eyes, she palmed my head, pushing me deeper into her wetness.

"Cum for me, baby," I told her, inserting two fingers inside of her, moving my fingers in and out at a slow-motion, causing her body to convulse.

"Kendrick, I'm cumming!" She moaned out as her sweet nectar filled my mouth.

I climbed on top of Lacey and inserted myself into her wetness. Once I found my rhythm, Lacey matched my every stroke until the both of us came together. When we finished, we both showered and threw some lounge clothes on. I decided to order some takeout, so neither of us had to cook. Lacey and I were sitting on the couch trying to find something to watch on TV. I looked over at Lacey, and she was so beautiful.

"Lacey, I love you so much," I told her.

"I love you too, Kendrick."

I heard my phone buzz, so I pulled it out, and I had a text message.

Sharee: *Kendrick, we need to talk.*

Me: *About what? And I thought I told you not to text me unless I text you?*

Sharee: *This is exactly what we need to talk about. I'm sick of you treating me like I'm only good enough to suck your dick.*

I had to read her message twice because this bitch was tripping. I couldn't respond like I wanted because Lacey was sitting right next to me.

Me: *I'll deal with this shit tomorrow. Don't hit my line again until I tell you where to meet me tomorrow.*

After I sent that text, I powered off my phone. That bitch had me fucked up.

"You good, baby?" Lacey asked.

"Yeah, I'm good. Just a work thing that I need to handle tomorrow."

She just nodded her head.

About twenty minutes later, the food was here. I went and paid for the food, and me and my girl chilled for the rest of the night.

Kendra

"Hey, baby. What you doing?" I asked my boyfriend, Anthony.

"I'm out chilling with the fellas. Wassup with you?"

"Nothing much. I just missed you, so I was going to swing through so we could chill."

"I'm not going to be home for a while, but I'll stop by and spend the night when I get done with the fellas."

"Okay, baby. I'll see you later. Enjoy your day," I told him before hanging up.

As soon as we hung up the phone, I threw on some leggings, a shirt, and a pair of sneakers and hopped in my car. For some reason, I had a weird feeling in the pit of my stomach about what Anthony said. I drove to Anthony's house, and when I pulled up, his car was parked in the driveway. Unless his ass was in the car with someone else, then he was in the house probably with a bitch.

I parked my car and used my key to get in. Anthony's keys were laying on the table, so I knew for sure that he was here. I walked up the steps, and the closer I got to his bedroom, the faster my heart started beating. I walked to the bedroom and turned the knob, and when I walked in, my heart damn near stopped at the vision of the light skin girl bouncing on Anthony's dick.

Something in me snapped, and I let out a scream before running over to the bed. I grabbed the girl off of him, then hopped on top of Anthony and started swinging on his ass. I wasn't too much worried about her because I wasn't sure if she even knew anything about me.

"You're such a fucking liar! How could you do this to me!" I yelled, hitting him repeatedly.

"Yo, chill the fuck out, Kendra!" he said, trying to get me off him.

He finally got me off him and pinned me to the bed, trying to calm me down, but all that did was infuriate me even more. I was just ready to get the fuck out of there and away from him. I broke loose and ran to my car. I locked the door and just sat there crying. Anthony came out and tried to get in the car, so I peeled off on his ass. Anthony had me all the way fucked up. I drove with no destination in mind.

I pulled up to Lacey's house and saw that my brother's truck was there, so I contemplated if I should go in or not. I didn't feel like hearing my brother's mouth, but

I needed someone to talk to. I parked my car and knocked on Lacey's door.

"Who is it?" I heard Kendrick ask.

"It's Kendra."

My brother opened the door, and I walked in with tears in my eyes.

"Kendra, what the hell is wrong with you? Why are you crying?" Kendrick asked.

"I caught Anthony cheating on me," I cried.

"Damn, sis, I'm sorry to hear that, but stop crying over that nigga. I'm gonna let y'all two talk. If you need me, I'll be in the room," he said before walking off.

I sat down and told Lacey what happened. After I chilled over there for a minute, I finally went home. Anthony was blowing my phone up, but I sent his ass to voicemail each time. When I got in the house, I sat down on the couch. I wasn't even sure why I was even tripping over his lame ass. I have been fucking around with

Anthony for six months, and I only started talking to him because he was so persistent. Every time he would see me, he would try to holla.

Since I was about my paper and he was spending, I was with it. If I could be honest, Anthony wasn't even that cute, but his money was long. Not as long as my brother's, but long enough to take care of me. I sat on my couch laughing like a crazy person at the way I acted in front of him and that bitch he was with. I played myself with that one because neither of them could care less about him getting caught cheating. I bet they will be fucking again.

It'd been two days since that shit happened with me and Anthony, and I haven't seen or heard from his ass, and I was cool with that. I was the type of bitch that would bounce back in no time. I didn't believe in working if I had a man in my life that I was fucking. I will never let a man lay up on me and not pay me.

I'd just pulled up to Lacey's apartment and knocked on the door. Lacey's brother, Liam, answered the door. I haven't seen Liam in a minute, but man, was he looking good. Liam was about six-two and nothing but muscles. He was chocolate, but his complexion was beautiful. He was rocking a sweatsuit, and I couldn't help but see the bulge in his pants.

"Hey, Kendra. Wassup with you? I haven't seen your fine ass in a minute," he said, licking his lips.

Damn, he's fine. "I know, it has been a minute. I'm good. Wassup with you?"

"I'm good, just chilling. All I do is work and go home."

"Where Lacey at?"

"She's in the shower. I came over to take my sister to lunch. You should come with us."

"A'ight, cool. I am hungry."

Lacey finally came out from getting dressed, and the three of us went to Bahama Breeze. The entire time that we were out, Liam just kept staring at me. We ordered our food and played catch up. Lacey was eating like she was six months pregnant, so I could only imagine how she's going to act when she started showing.

"So, are the two of you gonna eye-fuck each other all day?" Lacey asked, breaking me from my thoughts.

Liam chuckled at her comment. "Nah, but what I will say is, I didn't realize how fine Kendra was. But I will cut to the chase because I don't want y'all to beef, so I'm just gonna put it on the table. How would you feel about me talking to Kendra? I know chicks be having best friend codes and shit," he asked like I wasn't sitting here.

I was shocked that he was so blunt, yet I felt intrigued.

"Look, y'all grown, although I don't think you're her type," Lacey replied.

"Hello, I am sitting right here. And, Liam, I'm the one that you should be asking, not Lacey."

"I asked her first because if my sister didn't approve, I wouldn't come at you. But the food is here, so we can finish this conversation later."

After we ate, we drove back to Lacey's apartment. When we got there, I didn't bother to go in. I walked over to my car.

"I'll call you later, Lacey. I'm about to go take a nap." I got in my car, and when I looked up, Liam was walking over. I rolled the window down to see what he wanted.

"So you were just going to roll out without giving me your number?"

"You didn't ask me for my number, but here. Put it on your phone." I gave Liam my number, then peeled off.

A minute later, my phone started ringing. It was a number that I didn't recognize, so I knew that it had to be Liam.

"Yeah, just wanted to give you my number," Liam said into the phone as soon as I picked up.

"Thanks. I'll talk to you later. I have to deal with something," I told him as I disconnected the call.

When I pulled up, Anthony was parked in front of my house. I honestly wasn't beat to deal with him today, but since he's here, I guess I didn't have a choice. I got out of the car and walked to my door with Anthony on my hip.

"Kendra, I know you see that I've been calling you. Why haven't you answered my calls?"

I looked at Anthony and rolled my eyes. This nigga has a lot of nerve cheating on me, then expecting me to make myself available to him whenever he wanted me to be.

"Anthony, just come in so I can say what I need to say and be done with this." He looked at me like I was crazy, but obliged. "Look, Anthony, you and I are over. I won't deal with a liar and a cheater. At first, my feelings were hurt when I walked in and saw that bitch riding you. But after I left, I realized that there was no need to cry over spilled milk."

"So just like that, we're over?" Anthony quizzed.

"As quick as you blew me off for another bitch, just to get your rocks off, was the minute we were over. I'm not bitter, and I wish you the best. Now if you don't mind, I would like to take a nap," I told him.

"Kendra, that bitch doesn't mean shit to me. Don't do this to us," he pleaded.

"Well, in that case, Anthony, you should feel stupid for fucking up a good thing for someone that doesn't mean anything. You can stop begging because I won't change my mind. I'm not about to play myself again. Anthony, can you please go?"

"That's fucked up, Kendra," Anthony said before walking out the door.

After I locked my door, I went to go lay down. I didn't feel bad about ending shit with Anthony because he was the one that cheated on me. I was the type of chick that was about my money, and if all Anthony wanted to do was hook up and chill, I would have been cool with that because we wouldn't have been committed. Anthony damn near begged me to be in a committed relationship with him, and I told him, the first time he cheated on me, it would be a wrap, and I meant that shit.

Kendrick

I'd just pulled up to the block where this nigga, Anthony, trapped on. I wasn't planning on fighting him, but he and I needed to talk. When I walked up, he and a few other fools were out there shooting dice in the cold. I didn't see what my sister ever saw in this corny ass dude. It had to be the dick because he was corny and damn sure wasn't making the kind of bread that I was making.

"Yo, I need to holla at you for a minute," I stated. Anthony got up and we walked away from the crowd. "Listen, I don't typically get involved in my sister's business because she can handle her own, but what I don't play is seeing my sister crying over a nigga. I'm just here to tell you to stay the fuck away from her because she doesn't deserve to walk in her dude's house and catch him in some pussy.

"How could you be some dumb to fuck another bitch in a crib that your chick has a key to? That's some young fuck boy shit. Do what you want and who you want as long as my sister isn't the one getting fucked over. If you hurt her again, the next time you see me, we won't be talking," I warned before walking off. I didn't even give him a chance to respond.

I had shit to do. I had to make a New York run in a couple of days to handle some shit with my right hand, Troy. Troy and I went back to middle school. We lived on the same block, so before we knew it, we became tight as ever. Troy and I were both big bosses in the streets of Camden. Damn near all the corner boys that you saw worked for us.

Troy was a wild nigga out the door. Troy let you know what it was from the rip. If you fucked him over, you're one and done. He was the type that would put a bullet through your skull without thought. On the other hand, I was a little different. I didn't take any shit from anyone, either, but I'd kill you depending on the circumstance.

I was on my way over to his house now to go over the details about New York. Just as I was about to knock on the door, some chick was walking out. Troy stayed with a different chick in his bed.

"Yo, nigga, how many different chicks you got?" I asked when I walked in the door.

"I have enough to keep me satisfied with whatever I'm in the mood for."

"That's a lot of pussy."

"Just because you decided to wife up and settle down with one piece of ass don't mean you can clown me for leaving my options open."

"I'm not clowning you. Do you, bro. Lacey is special— not ten different bitches that I've fucked with, who could never compare to her, so I'm good. I'll admit, I had fucked up a few times since Lacey. I've been with her and with Sharee. But I only let Sharee suck me off because that bitch got a super throat."

"Damn, nigga. That must be some good ass head." Troy chuckled.

"It's the best, but that's all she offers, so I'm good on her. Honestly, I'm linking up with her tonight, but I'm cutting her off. Her simple ass texted me while I was chilling with Lacey. I told her ass never to contact me unless I contact her first. Not only that, but she's been making little comments about her wanting more, so now I'm done with her."

"Yeah, that shit ain't cool."

I chilled at Troy's spot going over what we needed to do when we got to New York before I bounced. I shot Sharee a text letting her know that I was about to ride through.

Me: *I'm about to stop by so we can talk.*

Sharee: *I'll meet you there in about ten minutes. I just left the hair salon.*

Me: *A'ight.*

I pulled up to Sharee's house and waited for her to get here. When she pulled up, I got out of the car. When she got out of the car, she was looking good as hell. She looked like she'd cut and dyed her hair red. The color fit her light complexion. Sharee was light-skinned with light brown eyes. She was only about five-five, but she was thick as hell with a fat ass.

"Hey, baby, wassup?"

"Wassup, Sharee?"

We walked into her house, and I sat on the couch. Sharee sat down next to me smelling good. She was making this harder than I planned for it to be.

"So what did you want to talk about?"

"You and I are done. You crossed the line, and that shit can't happen anymore. I asked you not to call or text me anymore, and you did it anyway. Not to mention that you have unreal expectations of me. You want more than I'm willing to give you."

"Look, I fucked up when I texted you because I was in my feelings. I promise I won't do that shit again. It just felt like you were slipping away."

"I am falling back, Sharee. You know that I have a girl, and I'm not risking that shit for no head, no matter how good it is," I told her straight up.

"Damn, that's all I was to you was some head?"

"Let's not pretend you don't know what it was. But this is what I'm talking about right here. You're acting like we have more than what we do. All that means is, when you get in your feelings again, you'll do something else stupid. And I can't afford to lose my girl over your shenanigans, so I'm good," I told her before standing up to leave.

"Kendrick, wait! I can't stop you from ending this, but since I'm the one that fucked up, at least let me give you a parting gift," she said, pushing me down on the couch.

I knew that I should have got up and taken my ass home, but my dick wanted to stay, so I listened to him and stayed. Sharee got on her knees and unzipped my jeans. Once my hard dick was free, she went to work, making me moan like a little bitch. I palmed her head and helped guide her up and down my shaft. I had my eyes closed, enjoying her warm, wet mouth as my dick touched the back of her throat.

My phone ringing caused me to open my eyes. I swiped the call without looking to see who it was. A couple of minutes later, I was cumming in Sharee's mouth.

Lacey

I'd just got home from organizing and furnishing the salon all day, and I was pretty tired, so I called Kendrick to ask him to bring me some curry chicken, rice, and cabbage since I didn't feel like cooking.

"Hello?" I said when the phone picked up, but he didn't say anything.

Just as I was about to hang up and call back, it sounded like I heard moaning. I put the phone closer to my ear and muted the TV.

"Fuck, Sharee, this shit feels good…Fuck, I'm about to cum," I heard Kendrick say.

My heart damn near stopped hearing Kendrick with another woman. I felt so many emotions at one time that I couldn't even think straight. I was hurt, angry, shocked, and disappointed. I felt like I was about to throw up, and that's exactly what happened. I ran to the toilet, hardly making it, before I was throwing up all over the place. I swear, this felt like a dream, and I had no clue how to deal with this type of hurt. My heart was racing so fast and hard. I couldn't even comprehend what I'd just heard. I just sat there for what felt like forever until Kendrick's voice pulled me back into reality.

"Babe, you good?"

Damn, how long was I really sitting here? I didn't even hear him when he came in. That's how spaced out I was, but anger took over my body, and I jumped up and charged him.

"Fuck you, Kendrick! How could you do this to me? I thought you loved me!" I yelled, swinging at him.

"Yo, chill, Lacey. What the fuck is wrong with you?"

"*You're* what's wrong with me, Kendrick! How could you cheat on me?" I cried, still hitting him. Kendrick was trying to block my hits and calm me down, but I was too pissed off for that.

"Lacey, what the fuck are you talking about?"

"Kendrick, just get out and go be with that bitch that you were just with!"

"I'm not going anywhere until you tell me what I was supposed to have done. You need to calm down while you're carrying my seed."

I knew that he was right, but I was so amped up. A few minutes later, I started to calm down a bit— at least enough to say what I needed to say.

"Who the fuck is Sharee, Kendrick?"

He was wearing a dumb ass look on his face. "Baby, Sharee is nobody. I don't give a damn about her. Look, baby, I'm sorry. I swear, I am. Just let me explain," he pleaded, but I wasn't beat to hear shit that he had to say.

"What I want you to do is leave! Please, just go!" I yelled, throwing my hands in the air.

This time, Kendrick didn't bother to put up a fight. He just walked out the door looking pitiful.

I walked over to the door and locked it. I laid there on the couch—crying—trying to process what I'd heard—trying to figure out why he would do this to me. I could never cheat on Kendrick, but clearly, when it came to me, he didn't have the same feelings. After laying on the couch for a little over an hour just sulking, I decided to call the one person that I knew I could talk to. A half-hour later, I heard my door. When I opened the door, it was my brother, Liam. As soon as he walked into the house, I hugged him tightly.

"Thanks for coming by."

"No thanks needed, sis. Now what's going on? You sounded a hot mess over the phone, and you don't look that hot in person, either."

"I heard Kendrick cheating on me."

"What do you mean, 'you heard him cheating on you'?"

"I called his phone, and he accidentally answered it, and I heard him tell some chick named Sharee that it felt good and he was about to cum."

"Oh, damn. I'm sorry, sis."

"I'm so hurt, Liam. How could he do something like this to me, especially while I'm carrying his child?"

"Look, Lacey, have a seat. Did you ask him about it?"

"No. When he came over, I just went off and started hitting him before making him leave."

"Well, how are you supposed to get an answer if you don't ask the question or allow him to explain himself?

All I'm saying is, give the man a chance to explain himself. If you don't like his answer, then do what you need to do for you. Y'all have a wedding coming up in a few months, so you're going to have to figure this out, sis."

"I can't marry him after this shit. Do you think I'm going to marry a man that could cheat on me while I'm carrying his baby?"

"So you're just going to throw your entire relationship away with a man you've been in love with since the eighth grade? No talking about it or nothing? If that's the case, Lacey, then marriage isn't for you. Marriage is hard work, and you can't just quit because things get hard. And just so know, any man that you deal with is capable of cheating on their pregnant fiancée. It happens all the time," he said.

"So you're telling me to forgive and still marry him?" I asked Liam, making sure I was understanding him clearly.

"That's not what I said at all. That's your choice; I can't tell you what to do in your relationship. What I said was, hear him out and go from there, and I also said that being married is hard work and you can't just drop him because you're mad about something. The two of you are about to have a child together, so y'all gonna have to be in one another's lives, no matter what. But it's for you to decide how you want to be in his life. You have to decide what you want to put up with. At the end of the day, the choice is yours, Lacey."

I listened to what Liam was saying, and I knew that he was right. I just wasn't ready to talk to him yet. It was too soon. As much as I loved Kendrick, I couldn't bear looking at him right now, nor any time soon. I just wanted to be left alone so I could process all this and figure out what I wanted to do.

"You're right. I'm just not ready right now. I need a little time," I told my brother honestly.

"Take your time, sis. This is your life that we're talking about. Just don't make a lifetime decision based on a temporary emotion."

"Thanks, bro. You're the best," I told him, hugging him.

"No thanks needed. I'm supposed to be linking up with Kendra in a few. Do you want to roll?"

"Nah, I'm good. I just want to be alone right now. Liam, you are free to date whoever you want, and I love my best friend to death, but just be careful with Kendra. She's kind of a gold digger and typically only dates street dudes who can take care of her."

"Thanks, sis, but I'm a big boy. I'm not the average man that she's used to. But I know one thing, if we get to the point where I put this dick in her, I'll change her entire life and outlook on things," he said, making me want to throw up in my mouth.

"That was too much information, but go ahead and enjoy yourself. I love you."

"I love you too, Lacey."

After Liam left, I went into the kitchen and made me a burger and some fries. After I ate dinner, I went into the bedroom, pulled out my phone, and saw that I had about thirty missed calls from Kendrick. I powered off my phone and cried myself to sleep.

***

The banging on my door caused me to jump up out of my sleep. I dragged myself out of bed and went to answer the door. I snatched the door open, and it was Kendra. I walked away from the door and went to use the bathroom. I walked out the bathroom, and Kendra was sitting on the couch.

"Kendra, why are you over here so early?"

"Lacey, it's noon, and I've been calling your phone all morning."

I looked over at the clock, and she was right. It was noon, and I felt like shit. "I didn't realize it was so late."

"Go shower and get dressed. We're going to go get something to eat."

"I don't feel like going out anywhere. I just want to go back to bed," I told her.

"Well, that's not an option, Lacey, so go get dressed."

I didn't bother to argue this time because I knew she wouldn't leave me alone. I went and showered and threw on some jeans and a shirt with a pair of Air Max. I put my hair in a messy bun and grabbed my phone and bag. We decided on Friday's because I had a taste for their whiskey-glazed wings.

As soon as we were seated, I ordered a strawberry lemonade and some wings. These wings were good as hell. I think I'm going to take an order home.

"Lacey, how are you feeling?"

I took a deep breath before answering her question. The truth was, I didn't want to talk about this. I didn't want to have to think about Kendrick right now, but I also knew that the situation wasn't going to go away.

"Kendra, how do you think I feel? I heard my fiancé cheating on me. He was enjoying the pleasures of another woman, and I had to listen to that shit. All I keep thinking about is how could he do something like this to me? We're supposed to be getting married in a few months, but I don't think I can go through with it. I can't be with a man that will cheat just because he can."

"Lacey, I know that you're hurt, but I think calling off the wedding without even talking to Kendrick first is a bit much."

"Kendra, what difference will it make if we talk before I call off the wedding? He cheated on me, and nothing will change that. I'm good right now. When I'm ready to talk to him, I will. Kendrick doesn't have the right to cheat on me, then still have access to me like he always has."

"He misses you, Lacey, and he's going crazy."

"Can we drop the subject? I really don't want to talk about this right now," I said, dismissing the conversation.

The table fell silent for a few minutes, and I was just ready to go back home and continue to be alone. Or go around to my shop and do a few odds and ends to keep my mind off Kendrick. I knew that it wasn't possible because I always thought about him day and night. Kendrick was my soulmate.

After we left from eating, I got in my car and drove to my salon. I heard my phone buzz, and when I picked it up, it was a text from Kendrick.

Kendrick: *Lacey, baby, I'm sorry for what I did, but I need to talk to you. I need to see your face and hear your voice. I want to check on my baby and see how my baby is doing. Please call me or text me back.*

I stared at Kendrick's text for about ten minutes. I was contemplating if I wanted to respond or not. No matter how angry and hurt I was, I missed him like crazy. Kendrick was my world, but I wasn't feeling like I was his. I knew that I didn't want to cut him out of our unborn child's life, but I just wasn't ready to deal with it right now. I decided not to respond. I placed my phone inside my bag and headed into the salon.

Kendrick

It's been two weeks, and Lacey still wasn't fucking with me. I felt sick to my stomach when I walked in that night and saw the hurt and tears on Lacey's face. I wasn't sure how she knew about Sharee until after I left and checked my phone and realized that I had answered the phone when she called. I feel like shit for what I did to Lacey. I wasn't even the type that cried over no chick, but Lacey wasn't just some chick. She was the woman I wanted to spend the rest of my life with. She was the woman that was carrying my seed.

I heard a knock on my door, breaking me from my thoughts, and when I answered the door, it was Troy.

"Nigga, enough is enough. You sitting around in the house pouting like a little bitch. I know that Lacey isn't fucking with you, but you're taking this shit too far now. This is fucking with our money. You're leaving this house today, even if I have to drag you out myself."

"I'm good. I'm not going anywhere today. I just want to be by myself, and what do you mean, 'this is fucking with our money'? Isn't that what you are for?"

"Just go shower and get dressed. I'm taking you out to get some air."

I wasn't beat to go out, but I knew this fool wouldn't leave me alone if I didn't. I got up and took a shower and threw some jeans and a shirt on with a pair of Jordans. I brushed my hair and put my jewelry on. This was something light, but I never left the house looking a mess. I grabbed my keys and phone and headed out the door.

We pulled up to Texas roadhouse for lunch, and I was kind of glad because I was starving. I haven't eaten much since that shit went down between me and Lacey. Troy was a pain in my ass, but he was my best friend for a reason. I was kind of glad to be out of the house. I guess I was tripping a bit. Sitting in the house sulking wasn't going to put me and Lacey back together. After we were seated, we ordered our drinks and food. While we were eating, my phone went off. I pulled it out, and it was a reminder that I'd set for Lacey's doctor's appointment. Suddenly, an idea popped into my head.

"Wassup? Why are you looking like that?" Troy asked.

"I just got a reminder that Lacey has a doctor's appointment tomorrow. So I'm going to go."

"I don't think that's a good idea for you to just show up after what happened."

"Look, I have the right to attend an appointment that pertains to my baby. If Lacey decides that she doesn't want to talk to me, then fine. I just need to lay eyes on her, and maybe if she sees me, she will talk to me," I told him.

"I don't know. That shit could backfire."

"Or, it could work. Either way, I'm going."

Troy didn't say anything else on the topic. Instead, he just finished eating his food. After we finished eating, he and I chilled back at my place for a couple of hours, smoking and drinking. After Troy left, I just sat and played my game when all I wanted to do was be with Lacey. To make things worse, Kendra wouldn't tell much about how Lacey was doing, either. She would only tell me that she was hurt and didn't want to have anything to do with me right now.

******

It was now the next day, and I was up getting ready for the doctor's appointment. I had to make sure I looked good. I haven't seen Lacey in weeks, so I had to make sure

I was looking good. I had on a burgundy sweater with some

black ripped jeans and my burgundy Timberlands. After I

put on my jewelry and brushed my hair, making sure the

waves were flowing, I sprayed some Polo Blue, which is

one of her favorite colognes of mine, and walked out the

door.

About twenty minutes later, I pulled up to the

doctor's office. I didn't see Lacey's car yet, so I tried to

park out of view. I didn't want her to not come in because I

was here. When I walked in, I went up to the front and

signed us in. I swear, I didn't know why I was so nervous.

All I could think about was Troy telling me that it was

going to backfire. I prayed like hell that didn't happen. The

last thing I wanted to do was piss Lacey off any more than

she already was.

Moments later, Lacey walked into the doctor's

office, and she didn't see me at first. Lacey was looking

good as shit. My baby had the prettiest chocolate-colored skin I ever saw. The pregnancy glow only made her even more beautiful. Lacey was about five-seven and was thick in all the right places. She was wearing her natural highlighted hair, which hung down to the middle of her back. I could feel my dick rising, causing a bulge in my jeans. She was wearing a pair of blue ripped jeans with a black sweater and some thigh-high heeled boots. My baby was looking good as hell.

"Hey, baby," I said, nervous as hell.

When she turned around, she looked like she saw a ghost. She went to speak, but her words got caught in her throat. "Kendrick, what are you doing here and how did you know I was going to be here?" she said a little above a whisper.

"Just because you're not talking to me doesn't mean that I wouldn't still show up to see what's going on with my baby."

"Kendrick, I didn't expect to see you here today, and to be honest, I'm not sure that I want you here. But since it involves the baby, I guess I can't keep you from being here. But I would like for you to respect my wishes and not speak to me about anything if it doesn't pertain to our baby," she said.

Lacey's words cut through my heart. I guess she was truly done with me. I was hurt, but I had to deal with it since I was the reason for this.

"Note taken," was all I could say.

Both of us took a seat but not directly next to one another. The room was silent and awkward. This wasn't something that I could handle. Not talking to Lacey was tearing me apart. I knew that I had fucked up, but the fact she could go two weeks without speaking to me or responding to my texts, then stand in my face and act like I'm not here in her presence, was a bit much for me. Maybe she shouldn't be the woman that I would spend the rest of my life with. Mad or not, we were grown, and the least we could do was talk about it.

I stood up, and she didn't even look at me.

"Yo, you win. I'm out. Just let me know when the ultrasound appointment is. Then after that, you won't have to worry about me until the baby is born. If you need anything, you know how to reach me," I told her before walking out of the doctor's office.

As I was walking out, I heard the nurse call her to the back. I got in my car and just sat here for a minute before pulling off. I wasn't even sure where I was going, but what I did know was, I wasn't going home. I decided to go see my mother. I needed someone to talk to. I knocked on the door, and my mom answered wearing night clothes, which was a little weird to me since she was usually up at sunrise, fully showered and dressed.

"Hey, baby. What are you doing here?"

"I just came over because I needed your advice. But why are you still in your Pj's at this hour?"

"I heard about what was going on with you and Lacey, and I was wondering when you were going to tell me yourself. And I'm still in my Pj's because I just wanted to chill today and have some time to myself, but wassup?"

"Mom, I don't know what to do. Lacey hasn't spoken to me in two weeks, and it's killing me. I popped up on her at the doctor's office today, and she made it clear that she didn't want me there and asked me not to talk to her unless it was about the baby. That shit hurt like hell," I expressed.

"Well, that was dumb for you to pop up on her knowing how she feels about you right now. Kendrick, you made this mess that you're in. All you had to do was keep that dick of yours in your pants, and you would still be getting married. That girl heard you with another woman months before she was about to marry you and while she's pregnant. You want her to pretend that it didn't happen?"

"I know that I messed up, Mom, but I thought we would have talked by now. What should I do, Mom? I'm losing it."

"You need to do a lot of ass-kissing and send expensive gifts and beg your ass off. Stand outside of her door and sing love songs to her. You're gonna have to go old school, son. That's the only way to get her to talk to you, unless she decides to talk to you on her own."

"Mom, now you know I'm not with all that corny mess. I'm not standing outside, singing outside no doors, and embarrassing myself," I told her.

"That's fine by me, Kendrick. I guess you don't want your woman back. I only have one more thing to say on the subject. If you're not willing to make a fool out of yourself for the woman that you love, then maybe you shouldn't get married. It's obvious that you're not ready to be someone's husband. I love you, son, but this is my chill time. You're gonna have to figure out how to get yourself out of this mess that you created. It's always a pleasure to see you, but I will talk to you later," my mom said, dismissing me.

This day wasn't getting any better.

I left my mom's house feeling defeated, so I decided to take my ass home. I guess I had lost my baby for good.

Kendra

I've been MIA for a minute because I was too busy hanging out with Liam. He was pretty cool. Just not like most guys that I typically dated. For one, he worked a nine to five. It's not that I had a problem with that. I'd just never been with a guy that wasn't in the streets.

I'd just pulled up to my house after coming from the market, and when I pulled up, I thought I was tripping when I thought I saw Anthony parked in front of my place. Sure enough, when I got out of my car, he got out of his.

"Hey, Kendra. Can we talk for a minute?" he asked.

I just stood there and looked at him like he was crazy because the nerve this man had blew my mind.

"Anthony, I can't think of anything that we would need to talk about, but since I'm in a good mood, I guess I can give you five minutes to say what you need to say."

"Well, are you going to let me come inside?"

"There's no need for that, and you're wasting your minutes."

"Kendra, I'm sorry that I fucked up with you, but I miss you like crazy. Can we just work it out? I swear, if you give me a second chance that I won't fuck up this time. I'll do whatever it takes," he stated.

I won't lie and say that I didn't give it any thought, but I just didn't feel like dealing with the bullshit right now. Besides, I wanna see where things could go with Liam.

"Look, Anthony, I appreciate you coming by, but at this time, I'm good. I've moved on already," I told him.

He stood there and looked at me like I was crazy before speaking. "Really, Kendra? So I guess I meant nothing to you since you could just move on within weeks. That's some hoe shit."

I let out a loud laugh because this nigga was tripping for real. "Anthony, you're something else. You're the one who fucked around on me while we were together. And now you're calling me a hoe because I said that I've moved on? You can think whatever you want to think. This conversation is over. Have a nice life," I told him before walking to my door.

"You know what, Kendra? Fuck you! I don't know why I even came over here," he stated before getting in his car.

All I could do was laugh because he was big mad. When I got in the house, I put my groceries away and sat on the couch. My phone ringing brought me from my thoughts. I looked at the number, and it was my brother. I let the phone go to voicemail because I didn't feel like dealing with him right now. Every time I talked to either Kendrick or Lacey, I had to hear about what was going on between the two, and it was starting to get on my nerves.

I wasn't trying to be an asshole, but their dilemma was between *them*. Lacey is either crying about how much she misses Kendrick, and all he does is cry about her not talking to him. I hated that I was in the middle of their crap. My phone rang again, and this time, it was Liam. A smile appeared on my face at the sight of his name. I've known Liam for years and never paid him any attention coming up, but he was fine as hell with a big personality.

"Hello," I answered with the sexiest voice I could muster up.

"Hey, baby. Do you have plans tonight?"

"Nope. I was just about to cook and chill."

"Do you mind if I come through?"

"Of course, you can come through. I'm about to shower and then start dinner."

"A'ight, cool. Go ahead and shower, and I'll help you make dinner," he said.

That only made me blush even harder than I already was, but I had to play it cool. "That sounds cool. I'll see you when you get here," I told him before hanging up the phone.

I walked into my bedroom and tried to find something cute, yet sexy, but not too sexy because I didn't want him to think I wanted to have sex. Although I wasn't too sure that I didn't. I know we haven't been talking for long, but doesn't knowing him since the eighth-grade count for something?

After my shower, I decided to put on some boy shorts and a tank top. I put my hair up in a ponytail and sprayed on some You're the One body spray from Bath & Body Works. Just as I was heading into the living room, I heard the door. I walked over to the door and let Liam in. Liam was wearing a black-tee and some jeans with a pair of black Air Max. When he walked in, he looked me up and down before licking his lips, making me blush. He pulled me in for a hug, and he smelled so damn good that I wanted to lick his neck.

"You smell good," he said before pulling back from the hug.

"Thanks, so do you. Are you ready to start cooking?"

"I sure am. What are we cooking?"

"Shrimp alfredo with broccoli," I told him.

"That's one of my favorite dishes."

The two of us walked into the kitchen to prepare the food. It was kind of sexy to watch him cook. After the food was finished, we sat down to eat.

I bit into the food, and it was delicious. Liam did the cooking while all I had to do was clean the meat and cut up the chicken and peppers. I was impressed that Liam could cook.

"Liam, this is delicious. Where did you learn how to cook so well?" I quizzed.

"Well, you're no stranger to my family, so you already know what type of parents I have. While they were busy drinking and partying, I still had to make sure that me and Lacey ate. So I just started cooking, and by the time I became an adult, Lacey and I was pretty good at cooking. Cooking is something that I love to do whenever I have free time. But running a shop doesn't leave much free time."

"I'm glad that I had the pleasure to taste your cooking."

"I'm glad that you enjoyed it. Do you mind if I ask you a personal question?"

"Sure, you can ask me whatever you like."

"Why do you feel like you have to fuck for money?" he asked bluntly, catching me off guard.

"First of all, I wouldn't say that's what I do, but what I will say is, ain't no nigga gonna lay on top of me and I'm struggling. So why should I work when I have niggas that's willing to pay for it?"

Liam ran his hand down his face before responding. "Kendra, I don't mean to come off disrespectful when I say this, but you're way too beautiful and smart to make a dumb statement like that. But there is one thing that you said that I do agree with, and that was, a nigga will be willing to pay for it. However, a man like myself will not pay for it. If I wanted a prostitute, then I would go get one.

"No man will ever take you seriously if you're wearing a price tag. I don't want to buy a woman; I want to earn my woman. I want to put in the time, work, and effort for mine. A real man gonna always make sure that his woman is taken care of, or die trying. Not only that, but you should want your own money and him to be honest. If the only way you're surviving is by a nigga, then you will always be struggling.

"I'm not trying to lecture you. I just care about you and would like to give you a better outlook on life. And to also let you know that if you're looking for me to take care of you, while all you do is lay on your back and give up pussy, that will never happen. And I'm not impressed because I can get pussy from anybody," Liam said.

I wasn't sure how I was feeling right now. I was angry and embarrassed. I know I've known Liam practically my entire life, but I didn't feel like we were cool enough for him to call himself judging me.

"Liam, you don't know me like that to come into my home and judge me."

"Look, Kendra. I know you're probably feeling some type of way about what I said, but I can assure you that I'm not judging you. I'm just telling you that you should want more out of life than selling pussy. And to make it clear, I'm not those niggas that you've dated. I'm a man."

My feelings couldn't have been more hurt. Before I knew it, tears had formed in my eyes. I sat here trying so hard not to let them fall, but my trying failed.

"I didn't know that's how you felt about me," I said, feeling a tear fall onto my face.

Liam scooted closer to me and wrapped his arm around me. "Baby, don't cry. I wasn't trying to hurt your feelings. I just wanted you to know your value. Please stop crying," he said, kissing my forehead.

I wanted to tell him to get off me since he was the reason why I was crying in the first place. But he smelled so good, and his hold was so strong that I didn't want him to let go. I laid on his chest and cried harder. I guess what they say wasn't a lie because the truth does hurt. I didn't realize how stupid I sounded saying what I said until Liam repeated it. After I was finished crying, I finally gathered up the words to respond.

"Thank you for being honest with me. No one has ever been that honest."

"No thanks needed. That's what a real man does. If a real man sees a broken woman, he builds her up and shows her what she's worth. Not let her stay broken. But, listen. I have to get ready to head out, but I would like to link up with you tomorrow when I leave work if you're up to it," he said before getting up from his seat.

I walked Liam to the door, and he stared at me as if he could see into my soul. He leaned down and kissed my forehead. Standing next to Liam, I truly felt short since he was every bit of six-two.

"I guess I will see you tomorrow," I told him before he left.

After Liam pulled off, I just sat on my couch in deep thought. I knew that Liam was right about everything that he'd said, but hearing that shit from my best friend's brother had me beyond embarrassed. *I wondered if she feels the same way about me?* I don't know why I turned out the way that I did because I grew up in a two-parent, respectable home, with a pretty great upbringing. What I did know was, I needed to change my way of thinking and figure out what I wanted to do with my life from here on out.

Lacey

I'd just got back from the salon, and I was just about finished and ready to have my grand opening. I wasn't sure how I was going to have a grand opening with all this Covid shit. I decided that I wasn't going to start working in the shop until this Covid shit passed, or after I had the baby. I didn't want to risk catching Covid-19, especially while I'm pregnant. Tomorrow, I was holding a virtual interview, so I could get a few people to work in the shop.

When I pulled up to my house, I got out of the car and walked into the house. No sooner than I sat down, the doorbell rang. I got up to answer the door. When I opened the door, it was a guy holding a large bouquet of red roses. I mean, it was huge.

"Hi, I have a delivery for a Lacey."

"Hi, I'm Lacey."

After I signed for the roses, I grabbed the huge vase that held the roses and shut the door. They were the most gorgeous roses I've ever seen. I pulled out the card and read it.

Lacey, baby, I know that flowers won't fix what I've done to you, nor will they ease your pain. But I figured I can start here just to say that I am truly sorry. I miss you so much, Lacey. I love you, baby...

Reading Kendrick's note brought tears to my eyes. It's been two months since he'd cheated on me, but I missed him every day, all day. I thought I was good with not being with him, but ever since the day he popped up to the doctor's visit, I couldn't seem to get him off my mind. He was looking good as hell, and he smelled even better.

Kendrick was tall and light-skinned with gray eyes. His hair had enough waves to get anyone seasick, along with a full, nicely trimmed beard. I wanted to call out to him when he walked off at the appointment. As crazy as it sounds, I was feeling bad for causing him to leave before the appointment began. I wanted to call or text on many days, but my pride wouldn't allow me to. Besides, I needed him to feel the way I felt and to prove a point that I wasn't going to be a woman to deal with a cheater.

I didn't have to, and I didn't want to. I'm not judging anyone who does accept it, but it's not for me. Maybe it was time for us to talk. We'd already spent thousands of dollars on a wedding that's due to take place in a couple of months. I didn't know what to do at this point. My heart still wanted me to marry him, but every time I think about what I'd heard on the phone, my mind canceled the thought of taking him back. I just sat here on the couch, staring at the beautiful roses, feeling lonely and horny. I put my feet up on the couch, and before I knew it, I had dozed off.

*****

I was awakened out of my sleep by the loud sound of music blasting through my window. At first, I thought that I was dreaming until it continued. Once I was fully awake, I got up and went to the window. I swear, I couldn't believe my eyes. It was Kendrick at the window, on his knee, holding a large boombox that was playing "On Bended Knee" by Boyz II Men.

"Darling, I can't explain

Where did we lose our way?

Girl, it's driving me insane

And I know I need just one more chance

To prove my love to you.

If you come back to me

I'll guarantee that I'll never let you go.

Can we go back to the days our love was strong?

Can you tell me how a perfect love goes wrong?

Can somebody tell me how to get things back

The way they used to be?

Oh, God, give me a reason I'm down on bended

knee..."

I opened the door with tears in my eyes. This was so romantic. Not to mention, he had an audience with all of my nosey ass neighbors outside recording with their phones. I knew that I would see this floating on social media. Any man that was willing to embarrass themselves to get their woman back must truly be sorry and in love. I walked over to Kendrick and hugged him tightly.

"Please, forgive me, baby. I'm sorry. I swear, I will never hurt you again. I love you, Lacey," he said into my ear, causing me to cry even harder.

I hadn't even noticed that rose petals were everywhere. I looked down and realized that we were standing inside of a heart that he made out of the rose petals. I looked into his eyes and leaned in to kiss him. The two of us shared a passionate kiss like it was just us two standing outside. I grabbed Kendrick's hand and led him into my apartment.

I wasn't sure what was going to happen from here on out, but what I did know was, I was ready to talk to him to see if we would be moving forward as husband and wife, or as co-parents. Kendrick sat down on the couch, directing me to sit next to him.

"Lacey, thanks for talking to me. I don't want you to say anything right now. I just want you to hear me out. Is that okay with you?"

I nodded my head yes, and he turned to face me before speaking.

"Lacey, there is no apology that I can give you that would take away the hurt that I've caused you. But I need you to understand that I am truly sorry for hurting you. I'm about to tell you something that you may not want to hear about that day, but I want to be honest and straight forward from here on out."

I looked up at him, not sure if I was ready to hear the details of that day, but I didn't say anything.

"The day you called, I was with a chick named Sharee. I went there to tell her that I was cutting all communication off with her because I was in love with you. When I was about to leave, she dropped to her knees and started sucking my dick. I knew I should have stopped her, but I got caught in the moment. I know that me telling you that she was giving me head when you called won't make you feel better, but that's what was going on."

"So have you ever fucked her before?"

"Yes, I have. It was mainly before you and I got together, but only once while we were together. But I swear, it will never happen again," he stated.

Hearing Kendrick admitting to having sex with someone while we've been together really hurt, although I'd already figured as much. A part from me wished he hadn't told me the truth, but the other part of me was glad that he was honest with me. I sat there quietly for a minute, not knowing how to respond.

"So now what, Kendrick? Am I just supposed to forgive you and still marry you in a couple of months?" I cried, not being able to control my tears.

"I would like for you to forgive and learn to trust me again. And, of course, I would love for you to still marry me, but at this point, it's not about what I want. I know that I fucked up, and I can never take back what I did. The only thing that I can do is try to get you to give me another chance and find it in your heart to trust that I will be a faithful husband."

"I'm not sure that it would be that easy for me, Kendrick. You took something from me. Before this incident came up, I trusted you with my life, my heart, and my soul…" The more I talked, the more I cried.

"Baby, I'm sorry, but please don't cry," he said, pulling me into his arms.

I laid my head on his chest and sobbed. I wanted to trust and believe him, but I wasn't sure if I could do it or not.

"We have a few months left before the wedding, and we've already spent mad money, but if you don't want to marry me right now, I understand. I don't want you to rush into something that you're not sure about. Maybe we can try going to pre-marital counseling," he suggested.

"That doesn't sound like a bad idea, but we're going to have to find one quickly if we're going to try to still get married in February."

"I'll clear my schedule until we find the right therapist."

The two of us sat on the couch talking for a bit. Kendrick ordered take out, and once we were finished eating, things seemed to get awkwardly silent.

"I meant to say thank you for the roses. They're beautiful, and so was your little concert outside my window. It was really sweet, not to mention, old school."

"You're worth that and so much more. I love you, Lacey, and no matter what happens with us, just remember I'll never love another woman the way that I love you. Baby, I appreciate you talking to me tonight and that you're willing to let me try to prove myself to you. I don't wanna overstay my welcome, so I think I should leave. Besides, I don't know how much longer I can sit here without pulling down your pants and eating that pussy."

I was already horny and missing Kendrick like crazy, so his statement only turned me on even more, but I didn't want him to know that, so I had to play it cool. I felt like a fool for even wanting him to touch me.

"Actually, I wouldn't mind if you stayed over tonight. I'm not going to lie. I don't want to have sex because I'm not ready for all of that just yet. Besides, I want us to go to the doctor together so we can get tested."

"If that's what you want, okay, but unless you were fucking someone while we were separated, then there's no need for all of that because I haven't fucked anybody. And even if I did, I would have strapped up. I don't play about my dick. Have you been with anyone?"

I thought about what I wanted to say. I knew I hadn't been, but this was my chance to get him back just a little so he could see how it felt. I knew I was being petty and spiteful, but I couldn't help myself. I just needed to cause a little doubt in his head.

"Kendrick, let's not talk about that. Let's just get tested to be sure," I stated.

Kendrick's facial expression made me wanna laugh so badly, but I needed to keep a serious face if I wanted my plan to work.

"Lacey, what the fuck are you trying to say? Are you telling me that you fucked somebody else?" he asked with a raised voice.

"Kendrick, that's not important right now. Let's just focus on moving forward."

Kendrick's jaw muscles tightened, and I could see his teeth clench as he tried to hold his anger. "Nah, fuck that, Lacey. You're gonna answer me right now. Who did you fuck while carrying my seed, Lacey?"

"Kendrick, you need to calm down."

"Don't tell me to calm the fuck down, Lacey. You need to tell me right fucking now who you been with."

I knew I was wrong, but his anger was bringing me joy. Now he would know how the fuck it felt to be hurt at the thought of someone besides him touching me.

"Okay, his name is Bob," I answered.

"Lacey, who the fuck is Bob? I can't believe you went out there on some hoe shit! Here I was, thinking that I had someone different, but you just like the rest of these hoes!" he yelled.

"So now I'm a hoe because we both had a sexual encounter that wasn't with each other? That makes me a hoe? At least I was single, but you, on the other hand, were an engaged man acting single."

"Look, I didn't mean to call you a hoe, Lacey. My bad. I'm just hurt and pissed right now. I just always thought that I would be your one and only. But I fucked up, so I guess I have to deal with it. Just tell me something. Who is he? Do I know him?"

"Actually, you do know him. You're the one who introduced us."

Kendrick's eyes closed, and he bit down on his lip. "I can't believe you would stoop that low and fuck someone that I know. Although his name isn't ringing a bell, where the fuck is he from, Lacey?"

"My drawer," I said, trying to hold in my laugh.

"What are you talking about, Lacey?"

"Kendrick, calm down. I'm talking about my toy that you bought me," I said, bursting out into laughter. I was laughing so hard that I had tears rolling down my face. I swear, it felt like I was about to throw up from all the laughing that I was doing.

"Lacey, that shit ain't funny. You almost gave me a heart attack," he stated.

"Well, that's how I felt listening to another woman pleasure you. It felt like death, and I don't ever want to feel that way again," I told him seriously.

"And you won't. I swear, I will never hurt you again. Baby, if you felt anything close to what I just felt, then I'm even more sorry than I already was, and I didn't think that could be possible," he admitted.

"Well, it was like no pain I've ever felt before."

Kendrick didn't say anything. Instead, he moved in closer and kissed me passionately. I deepened the kiss and let out a moan. Kendrick took my hand and led me into my bedroom.

Kendrick

It felt so good to wake up next to my baby. Lacey was still sleeping, so I just laid here in bed staring at her. Lacey's chocolate-colored skin was so beautiful. After Lacey had me feeling like the world had come to end and gave me a taste of my own medicine, I took her into the bedroom and ate her pussy so good that it was like I'd sucked the soul out of her. I missed her like crazy. We didn't have sex because I didn't feel like I had earned it just yet. I had some ways to go before I would get there again. As horny as I was, I needed to make sure I kept her satisfied, in whatever way she needed me to satisfy her, until she was ready to take the next step.

While she laid there looking pretty, I thought back to my conversation with my mom, and I was glad that I took her advice and went old school to prove my love. That was out of my norm but most definitely worth it. I knew that niggas was going to think I was soft once that shit went viral, but I dared a nigga to try me, and I would still bust a cap in their asses. It was so many nosey ass people recording me, so I knew that it would be on any site that you could think of.

I leaned over and kissed her forehead, and she opened her eyes.

"Good morning, beautiful."

"Good morning," she replied.

"I'm sorry, I didn't mean to wake you. It's just that you're so beautiful," I told her, causing a smile to appear on her face.

"Thanks, baby."

She got up to use the bathroom, and I just laid there thinking about how grateful I was for having a woman like Lacey. I don't know how I could have been so stupid and cheated on her. If I didn't know anything else, I knew that I would never do anything to hurt her again. If she did take me back, it would just be the two of us until death did us apart.

Lacey walked back into the bedroom, still naked from last night, making me want to taste her. I pulled Lacey down on the bed and dived in between her thighs. I swear, she got wet instantly, filling my mouth with her sweet juices. After making her cum, the two of us laid here on the bed as she caught her breath.

"Baby, if it's not too soon for me to ask, I wanted to know if I could take you out to eat and maybe take you shopping?"

She looked at me for a moment before answering. "I don't have a problem with that."

"A'ight, well, let's get dressed so we can grab some breakfast before we get the day started."

*****

About an hour later, we pulled up to Sabrina's Café in Collingwood. After we were seated, both of us ordered French toast, sausage, and cheese eggs with a glass of orange juice.

"Kendrick, I don't know what's going to happen with us, but I wanted you to know that it feels nice having you back around. I've missed you so much and wanted to reach out to you plenty of times, but the hurt that I felt outweighed how much I missed you."

"Lacey, I don't know what it will take to help ease your pain, but what I do know is, I will do whatever it takes to make and keep you happy. I feel so stupid for stepping out on you. I was so lost without you. I'm not going to lie, but the day at the doctor's office hurt me to the core. I thought that we were completely over. That was something that I just couldn't handle. I couldn't eat or sleep. I'm just glad to be able to look at you because not seeing you or talking to you was killing me."

"Kendrick, I honestly didn't even think that I would ever come close to forgiving you. I still don't know what's going to happen, but I do know that I love you enough to try for the sake of us and our newborn."

Honestly, that was all I needed to hear was Lacey saying that she was willing to try. I leaned over and kissed Lacey deeply. The kiss was interrupted when the waiter walked over to the table to bring the check over. After we left the restaurant, we headed to the Cherry Hill Mall to do a little shopping. Hours later, we pulled up to Lacey's apartment, and I got out of the car to carry her bags in the house.

"Lacey, thanks again for allowing me to try to prove myself."

Lacey just nodded her head in agreement. "Are you coming in?" she asked.

"Nah. I'm going to give you a little headspace, and I'll text you later. If you want me to come back, then you already know that I will be here. I don't want to rush things or make you feel rushed."

"I like the sound of that. Kendrick, thanks for last night and today."

"No thanks needed. I'm the one who should be saying thank you. I love you, baby," I told her before walking to my car.

"I love you too, Kendrick."

I got in the car smiling and pulled off.

Liam

I'd just got to the shop, ready to start my day. I knew today was going to be a long yet exciting day for me. I was doing a major customized bike today. It was going to take some time, but it would be well worth it. Not only would this be a good look for my shop, but I would also make a shit load of money just off this one bike. As soon as I walked into my office, my phone rang, and when I looked at the number, it was Kendra.

"Hey, baby. Wassup?" I answered on the first ring.

"Hey, baby. I just wanted you to know that I'm on my way, but I'm stuck in traffic on 42. It was a bad accident."

"Damn, I hope everyone is good."

"I don't know, baby. Someone is stuck in their car, and they are about to saw them out."

"All we can do is pray. I'll see you when you get here. I'm about to get started on this bike. It's gonna take all day."

"Okay, I'll let you get to work."

With that, we ended the call.

The name is Liam Daye, and as you already know, I'm Lacey's older brother. I own a car shop, but I mainly specialized in bikes, motorcycles, Harleys, four-wheelers, and cannons. Ever since I was a little boy, I liked to fix shit and draw. Not to mention, I had a thing for cars and bikes, so I knew I would own my own shop one day. I bought this shop when I was eighteen years old, right after high school.

I took a business class and an automotive program. By the time I had my degrees in both, I was ready to work. My business took off pretty quickly because I used to do little shit for the guys from the hood. So once I was official, they continued to bring their bikes and cars to me, which helped build my clientele.

I sat my things down, grabbed my designs for the bike, and headed into the garage.

"Hey, boss."

"Wassup, Richardo?"

"Not much. I see we have a full day today."

"Yes, we do. I'll see you later this evening."

When I got into the garage, I got right to work. I had to draw a dragon on both sides of the bike, from one end of the bike to the other. Then I had to color it in and add fire coming out of the dragon's mouth. When I was finished with this bike, it was going to be fire. A few hours later, and I was finally finished with drawing the dragon on the first side of the bike. I was about to grab a bottle of water before I got started on the second side.

The garage door then opened, and it was Kendra.

"Hey, baby. I brought you something to drink," Kendra said, handing me a bottle of water.

"Thanks. I was just about to grab a bottle. Are you just getting here?"

"No, I've been here for a couple of hours, but we were pretty busy upfront. Plus, I didn't want to distract you. Oh my God, this is nice. This bike is going to be fire when you get finished. I love it already."

"Thanks, babe. Wait until I add the color."

"Let me get out your way and get back to work."

I hired Kendra as my assistant about two weeks after we had that talk about her future. I have liked Kendra for years, but she was a little too wild for my liking. However, that day I saw her at my sister's crib, I decided to shoot my shot with her. I figured I could try to help her see that it was more to her than what she saw in the mirror.

Kendra was light-skinned with light grayish-colored eyes. She was perfect in size with a big ass and perky breasts, and she was about five-six. She always had great taste when it came to fashion. I wanted her to see how it felt to bring home her own money that she didn't have to have sex for. Since she's been here, she'd been doing a great job. She and I spent most of our free time together, and I was truly feeling her. I was going to wait a little longer, but I think I was going to make it official with Kendra sooner, rather than later.

We haven't had sex yet, but we have kissed and been on plenty of dates. Before we crossed that line, I wanted us to get tested, and I wanted her to get on birth control before we started sexing. As long as she was straight, I didn't plan on using a condom with her because I was allergic to condoms, which is why I was particular about who I slept with. I used non-latex condoms, but I didn't like the feeling.

*****

It was the end of the day, and I had finally finished the bike. I knew it was going to be hot, but I wasn't expecting this look. I pulled out my phone so I could take pics, then I called Mike to let him know that the bike was ready. A half-hour later, Kendra came out to the garage to inform me that Mike was here. While she was here, she took a look at the finished bike and smiled.

"Wow, baby, this is impressive," she said, kissing me on the lips.

After our kiss, we walked inside of the building so I could bring Mike out to see the work.

"Yo, Liam, wassup? I'm ready to see what you did with my baby," he said, rubbing his hands together.

"A'ight, let's go check her out," I told him, leading him to the garage.

When we walked into the garage, I watched Mike eye the bike, and his eyes lit up like a kid in the candy store.

"Yo, this shit is fire, Liam! You outdid yourself with this one."

"I'm glad that you like it."

"Like is an understatement. I now have the hottest bike around."

"Well, I have one more thing to show you that I think you're going to love." I powered on the bike so he could see how realistic the fire would look while riding.

"Yooo, Liam, how the fuck you make this look so real!"

"This is what I do," I told him, tooting my own horn.

Mike pulled a wad of money from his pocket and handed it to me.

I looked at him with a funny look because I could already tell that this was more than I was charging him. "How much is this?"

"It's two hundred grand. I gave you extra for a tip and to say thank you for all the new pussy I'm about to get because of this bike. Enjoy it because you deserve it."

I just shook my head and thanked him. That was some of my best work, and I was proud of myself. After making sure that everything was good with the shop, I headed home so I could shower and get dressed because I decided I was in the mood to celebrate. I hit up Lacey and Kendrick to see if they wanted to join, and they said yeah. I was so glad that the two of them were working it out because my sister was miserable without him as he was without her.

Kendra

"Oh, God, Liam, don't stop!" I moaned as Liam slowly stroked in and out of my wetness.

Liam had made love to every inch of my body. He was hitting spots that I wasn't aware that I had. Liam began to kiss me passionately. I couldn't describe the feeling that I was experiencing because no man had ever made me feel like this.

"Shit, Kendra, this pussy feels so good. You about to make me cum," he said, looking me in my eyes, never missing a stroke.

I bit down on my bottom lip and started winding my hips in a circular motion as I embraced Liam's strokes.

"Oooh, Liam, I'm about to cum…" I moaned as my eyes rolled into the back of my head. My body convulsed, and it felt like I was having a mini seizure.

"Fuck, Kendra, I'm cumming!"

After we both came, Liam just laid inside of me, catching his breath. Before rolling over onto the bed, he kissed my lips. I knew we had only been dating for a couple of months, but I was falling for Liam pretty hard.

Liam gave me butterflies every time that I was around him. He was the first man that treated me like a person and not a piece of ass. All these years I was selling myself short, thinking that I was the one in control, but those men that I was sleeping with only wanted one thing to begin with, and I was giving it to them just because they had a little money. Now that I have Liam, I would never go back to that life.

"I love you, Kendra," Liam said, breaking me from my thoughts.

"I love you too, Liam," I replied, not even having to think about it.

I leaned over and passionately kissed Liam. I climbed on top of him and deepened the kiss. I felt his thickness harden, so I guided his thickness into my wetness. We made love and explored one another's body until the wee hours of the night.

******

The next morning when I woke up, I made my way to Liam's kitchen to see what he had in the fridge so I could make him breakfast in bed. After searching the fridge, I found the ingredients I needed to make breakfast. A half-hour later, I was heading upstairs to let Liam know that breakfast was ready, but on my way up, he met me on the steps.

"Hey, baby. I was wondering where you snuck off to."

"I'm sorry. I wanted to make you breakfast. I was headed up to get you."

"I'm glad that you cooked. I'm starving," he said, placing a kiss on my lips.

The two of us sat and ate breakfast. I made pancakes, maple turkey sausages, and cheese eggs. After the two of us ate, we ended up back in bed sexing one another for the past hour until we fell back to sleep. I could get used to being with Liam long-term.

*****

When I woke up, Liam wasn't laying next to me. Instead, there was a note on his side of the bed.

Hey, baby,

I'm sorry that I wasn't there when you woke up. I didn't want to wake you. I should be finished in a couple of

I read the note twice, smiling each time I read it. I rolled around on the bed, then kicked my feet like a happy kid who just had cake. I looked at my phone to see what time it was, and it was a little after two. I got up so I could head home and could chill for a minute before going out with Liam tonight. I had to make sure I was super cute.

As soon as I got home, I decided to do a little cleaning. I had been staying the night at Liam's house for the past three days, neglecting my home. By the time I was finished cleaning, I had just enough time to get cute. I got into the shower and lotioned my body. I still had no clue what I was wearing tonight. I walked over to my closet and went through my clothes. I decided on a gray body-con dress with a pair of heeled burgundy booties. I grabbed my burgundy Birkin bag and placed it on my bed. I was going to wear my hair in a messy bun but decided to put some large bouncy curls in it.

After I was finished doing my hair, I put light makeup on and sprayed myself with some perfume. I looked in the mirror, and I was satisfied with my look. Just as I was on my way into the living room, I heard the bell. I got excited at the thought of seeing Liam. When I opened the door, I caught an attitude seeing that it was nobody but Anthony's lame ass.

"Damn, Kendra, you're looking good as shit. You must have known that I was coming through," he said, smiling hard and looking dumb.

I rolled my eyes at his whack ass comment. "Anthony, why the hell are you at my house? You know better than to pop up like we're cool like that," I snapped.

"You haven't answered my calls, so I decided to slide through and see what's up with you. I know you miss me."

"If I missed you or wanted to talk, you wouldn't be on my block-list, and I would have come to see you. Now if you don't mind, can you leave and never come back?"

Right at that moment, Liam's fine ass walked up.

"Hey, baby. You good?"

"Yes, I'm great, now that you're here. This young man was just leaving," I said with a wide smile.

Anthony stepped aside to let Liam in. As soon as Liam walked in, I closed the door, leaving Anthony standing on the porch.

"Who the hell was that clown?"

"The dude, Anthony, that I told you about."

"Y'all straight?"

"I'm good. I'm sure that his feelings are hurt, but he'll be okay."

"Well, enough about him. We need to get going. We have reservations at 7:15. Here, bae. These are for you," he said, handing me a bouquet of red and white roses.

I hadn't even realized that he had them in his hand when he walked up.

"Aww, babe, thank you so much. They are so pretty," I told him.

I was glad that they were already in a vase because I damn sure didn't have one. I never saw myself as a romantic type of woman that did flowers, yet here I was, feeling all mushy inside. I kissed Liam on the lips before we headed out the door.

About an hour later, we pulled up to Kelsey's in Atlantic City. When we walked in, the hostess took us to our seats. After ordering our drinks and food, I took the place in, and I was feeling the vibe. This was my first time here, but if the food was good, this wouldn't be my last.

"Baby, I brought you out here tonight because I wanted to talk to you about something," Liam said, gaining my full attention. "We've been seeing each other for almost two months now, and I'm really feeling you. So, I was wondering how you felt about us being exclusive? Like, just you and me. I would like to see where things can go with us."

I knew that we were getting pretty close, but I didn't think that we were "exclusive" serious. Not that I was seeing anyone else anyway, and I never bothered to ask him if he was seeing anyone else, either. I had to admit, it didn't sound like a bad idea. We did just admit that we loved one another.

"I think I would like that," I told him.

"I think I would like that too."

The two of us shared a kiss at the table until the waiter brought over out meals and then check a little later. Liam paid for the check, and the two of us left out the restaurant and got in the car. After we left the restaurant, we went to the Borgata Casino and gambled for a little bit. Once we were tired of gambling, Liam got a room at the

Borgata where we spent more time getting it in than we did

sleeping.

Lacey

Kendrick and I had just pulled up to the doctor's office. I was a little excited because we were about to have an ultrasound, and the doctor said since I was a little over four months, that it was a possibility that we could find out what we were having today. Of course, I wanted a little princess, while he wanted a little man to play football with. I walked into the doctor's office and signed in.

"So are you excited? Today just might be the day," Kendrick asked.

"I'm a little excited at the thought of finding out, but I'm trying not to get my hopes up too high in case we don't find out today."

Before he could respond, we got called to the back. Kendrick grabbed my hand as we headed to the back. I laid on the table and lifted my shirt up.

"Good morning. Are y'all ready to see your little one?" the doctor asked.

"Good morning, and yes, we're ready," I replied.

"This may be a little cold," she stated as she put the machine on my baby bump.

Kendrick stood on the side of me holding my hand the entire time. I was in such awe seeing my baby on the screen, and the heartbeat was loud and strong.

"Doc, do you think we will be able to find out what we're having today?" Kendrick asked excitedly.

"It's a little early by a few weeks, but not impossible. Let's take a look."

I squeezed Kendrick's hand, and when I looked up at him, he was smiling from ear to ear. His smile was starting to turn me on, so I focused on the screen.

"Okay, let's take a look. It looks like you will be having a little girl," she stated.

I was so excited knowing I was having a little girl. "Oh my God, we're going to have a daughter, Kendrick!"

"Oh, Lord. Now I have to live with two nagging women," Kendrick said playfully.

I punched his arm lightly while smiling. "Like cleaning up after two guys is any better."

The doc laughed as the two of us playfully went back and forth. "Y'all are so cute, and you're all finished," she said as she wiped the gel off my stomach.

"Thanks. This woman right here is my world, and I can't wait to spoil our little princess when she arrives," Kendrick said, staring into my eyes.

"I can tell that she means the world to you. It's nice to see people that are still in love."

I thought about what she said, and it just made me think about how in love I was with Kendrick. I know we have our ups and downs, but I couldn't picture my life without him.

After we left the doctor's office, we went to get something to eat. On the ride there, I thought about how good things were with Kendrick and me ever since we started therapy. We have a great therapist, and we both liked him, especially because he's a man of God but still kept it real. I've still gone back and forth about whether I wanted to push the wedding back or continue with it in February.

I haven't told Kendrick just yet, but I decided to still marry him. I guess I should tell him so we can get this thing on the road. We only had two months left with plenty to do. I needed to call the wedding planner back and let her know that everything was still moving forward.

We soon pulled up to Collingswood Diner. The two of us sat down and ordered our food.

"What's on your mind, babe? You've been pretty quiet since we left the doctor's. Aren't you excited that you're gonna have someone to play dress up with?" he asked with a smile.

"I'm more than excited. Finding out what I'm having just made the pregnancy feel even more real. I was quiet because I was just thinking about us, and there's something I wanted to talk to you about."

"Wassup, babe? Talk to me."

God, this man is sexy as hell, and that smile made me melt every time he flashed those pretty teeth of his.

"Well, after some long thinking and our great therapy sessions, I was thinking that we could still get married on Valentine's Day. I mean, I can't see my life without you in it, and if I could be honest, I don't want to even imagine it. Kendrick, I've been in love with you since I laid eyes on you when I was thirteen years old. And I love you even more now than I did then, and I didn't think that was even possible."

"Lacey, I love you more than anything in this world. I would lay down my life for you as well as take a life for you. You may have forgiven me for hurting you, but I haven't forgiven myself yet, and I don't know if I ever will. What I did was stupid, and I feel like shit every day for what I did to you. But I swear, Lacey, that I have learned my lesson, and I will never stick my dick in another woman as long as I live—not unless you want to have a threesome or something."

I looked at Kendrick with a side-eye.

"I'm just saying, babe. I'll only do it if you request it."

All I could do was shake my head at this fool. "Look, Kendrick. I'm not sure if I would say that I have completely forgiven you, but what I will say is that I'm working very hard on it. I'm working hard to move forward. I believe that you are sorry for what you have done. But I need you to know that if it ever happens again, we're through. I don't ever want to feel that pain," I told him, feeling a tear trying to fall. I quickly wiped my eyes, refusing to let a tear fall.

"Baby, I'm sorry, but please don't cry. I swear, it will never happen again. I love you, Lacey. Now let's get this wedding planning going so I can make you my wife, and let's get out of here so we can celebrate our princess."

"And just how will we be celebrating?"

"Well, since you can't drink, and I don't want to tempt you, I think that some good ole loving would be the best option."

"You are so nasty, but I'm going to have to agree with you, so let's get out of here so we can celebrate."

*****

It's been two weeks since I found out that I was having a girl, and it seemed like I got more and more excited every day.

The shop opened up last month, and everything was going pretty good so far, especially with the pandemic going on. I didn't actually do hair there yet, but I stopped in to make sure that everything was running smoothly. I didn't want to risk the chance of catching the virus and putting the baby at risk.

Today, I only came to take inventory. While I was at the shop doing my inventory, it was two chicks in my chairs talking.

"Sharee, are you and Kendrick really over?" the one girl asked.

My heart dropped hearing the name Sharee. I wondered if they were talking about my Kendrick?

"Yup. I haven't seen or heard from him since the day he left my house. I feel so stupid. He came over to tell me he was done with me because he was in love with his girl, and I still sucked that nigga off, but then he bounced like I wasn't shit. I tried calling him a few times, but I think he blocked me or changed his number."

"Damn, that's crazy because that nigga fine as hell, and his money is long."

"Girl, yes, but he ain't never spent any money on me. I guess you have to be his girl to get his money," the girl, Sharee, said.

"Bitch, your ass is crazy because ain't no way I'm fucking a nigga like Kendrick and not gon' make him come up off no money," the other girl said.

"It wasn't about the money when it came to him. I really liked him, but I guess I was only good enough to suck him off."

My heart was beating so fast, but I was happy to know that he wasn't lying about what he told me, but I was mad overhearing about this bitch and my man.

"You know, that's what happens when you're the side chick," I chimed in.

"Excuse me?" she said.

"I think you heard exactly what I said. Y'all side jawns don't have no chill. You said that he came to break it off, but nope. You tried to make him change his mind by sucking his dick."

"I don't see how what I'm doing is any of your business," she said, rolling her eyes.

"I think it has everything to do with me when you're talking about *my* man in *my* shop. I'm sure you knew what you were doing when you came in here and started talking about him in front of me. I doubt that this was a coincidence."

The entire shop now had all eyes on me, and I felt stupid for even allowing myself to feed into her messy ass. Not to mention, this was my place of business, and I'd just brought my personal life into my work life.

"Chile, don't flatter yourself if you think we came up here to spend our money just to talk about your nigga," the other girl said.

Before I could respond, and just when I thought things couldn't get any worse, Kendrick walked in the door.

"Hey, babe, you left your phone..." But his words trailed off when he saw the look that was on my face.

"Kendrick?" Sharee had the nerve to say.

"Sharee? What the fuck are you doing here? I know you better not be in my fiancée's shop starting no shit."

"Babe, I'm good. These two just decided to come to my shop and talk about the dick-sucking you got from her the last time you saw her. But it's all good, and I should have never given her the satisfaction. Thanks for bringing my phone. I didn't even realize that I had left it."

"Yo, that's fucked up, Sharee, and after today, don't come back to this shop before I have you dealt with," Kendrick said to Sharee.

"Damn, it's like that, Kendrick? Wow, I can't believe you," she said, sounding hurt.

Kendrick was about to respond, but I stopped him. The two of us walked outside. I could tell that Kendrick was worried about my feelings, and the fact that shit was thrown in my face when I was barely over it.

"Baby, I'm sorry. This was the last thing that I needed to happen while we're still trying to get past it," Kendrick said.

"Look, baby. At first, I was pissed, but I'm good now. I'm just going to finish my inventory, and I'll be done in about an hour," I told him, kissing him.

I wasn't even gonna trip and take it out on my man for her fuckery. Even though if he never would have fucked her, we wouldn't be here. But I truly am trying to get past this.

"Baby, I love you so much," he told me.

"I love you more, baby."

I walked back into the shop with my head held high like ain't shit happen. I refused to let that bitch win. I finished doing my inventory. Once I was finished counting, I walked into my office to put my order in. I grabbed my belongings so I could leave. Just as I was about to walk out the door, Sharee walked up to me and asked if we could talk. I wasn't sure what she wanted, but I figured I would hear her out. I gave her a head nod, letting her know she could speak.

"I'm sorry for coming to your work place being petty. I just wanted to know who you were and what you looked like. I know that you probably don't want to hear this coming from me, but the one thing I know is that Kendrick loves you. He's always made that clear. I should have never fucked with him knowing how he felt about you. I feel bad, and I'm woman enough to say that I was wrong, and I'm sorry," she stated.

"Apology accepted. Just don't let it happen again, and don't feel bad. Do better. But I appreciate the apology. Have a nice day, Sharee," I replied before walking to my car.

Liam

"Do you think he would like this?" Lacey asked, holding up a wedding band for Kendrick.

"Honestly, sis, I think that nigga would wear aluminum foil as long as you're the one giving it to him," I told her, causing her to laugh.

"I swear, you're so stupid, Liam."

"Nah, this ring is hot. This is something that I would wear," I told her honestly.

"Speaking of rings, how are you and Kendra making out? Do you see marriage in your future?" my sister asked.

"To be honest, Lacey, I love Kendra a lot, and I could see myself spending the rest of my life with her. I don't know when, but you know me. If I want something, I'm going to go for it. These few months with Kendra has been some of my best months ever in life. Kendra has come a long way."

"I'm glad that she found someone like you. She deserves it, and I'm glad you're the man that's showing her what she's worth. I can see the change in my best friend, and I love it. I'm also happy that you found someone to love you for you."

"Thanks, sis. I feel the same way about you and Kendrick. I couldn't think of a man better than him to call my brother-in-law."

"Thanks, bro. I love you, Liam, and thanks for always being here for me."

"I love you too, Lacey."

After Lacey finished paying for the ring, the two of us went our separate ways. I had to go past the shop to do payroll. When I walked into the shop, Kendra was on the phone with a customer looking good as shit. I was ready to take her into the office for a quickie.

"Hey, baby. You looking extra good today for some reason."

"Thanks, babe. I missed you while you were gone," she replied.

"I missed you too. Why don't you come to my office so I can show you just how much."

Kendra licked her lips before leaving the desk and following me into the office. As soon as we got in the office, I didn't waste any time hiking up her skirt and bending her fat ass over my desk. After we both came, we both wiped off and went back to work. After I was finished doing payroll, Kendra and I left for the day. I had a huge surprise for her and just hoped that I wasn't overstepping or moving too fast.

"Baby, I have a surprise for you."

"You have a surprise for me? What is it?"

"Kendra, do you know what a surprise is? If I told you what it was, then it wouldn't be a surprise."

Twenty minutes later, we were at our destination. She was looking around, trying to figure out why we were on the same street as my sister's salon.

"Babe, why are we at Lacey's shop?"

"Just relax," I told her, walking up to the building five doors down from Lacey's hair shop.

I pulled out a set of keys and opened the door. The two of us walked in holding hands. Kendra's eyes lit up at the huge, empty yet beautiful space.

"This is beautiful, but what is it?"

"It's your new clothing store or boutique. Whatever you want to do with it," I told her.

She had a confused look on her face. "Liam, what are you talking about?"

"I know how much you love fashion, and you can dress your ass off, so I thought, what better way to step out on your own than to own your own clothing store? You don't owe me anything. Everything is in your name, so if we don't work, you can still keep it. I just want to see you win."

"Oh my God, Liam, this is the nicest thing anyone has ever done for me! Thank you so much. I don't even know what to say right now," she said. Her voice was laced with emotion. She turned to face me and hugged me tightly. "Baby, thank you so much," she cried.

"No thanks needed, babe. I got you. Just know that Kendra," I assured her.

Once she got her emotions in check, we took a tour of the place. The more we walked around checking the place out, the more emotional she got. I had shot my sister and Kendrick a text, telling them to meet us at Longhorn at 6 PM for dinner tonight. I didn't tell them why. I just told them that we were celebrating something great.

After we left the building, we both went to my house to get dressed for dinner. Kendra has been staying at my house at least three to four times a week, so she had plenty of clothes there. An hour later, we pulled up to Longhorn. When we walked in, Lacey and Kendrick were already there. The hostess took us to our seats, and we sat down.

"Hey, y'all, wassup? Kendrick said.

"So what are we celebrating?" Lacey asked, not wasting any time.

"Go ahead, baby. Tell them the news."

"My baby bought me a boutique because I love fashion, so he thought that I should sell clothes!" Kendra blurted excitedly.

"Oh my God, Kendra, I'm so happy for you. I think a clothing store would be perfect for you. So where's the store? Is it in Camden?" Lacey asked.

"I'm glad that you asked. It's like, five doors down from your hair shop."

"I know you're lying! It has to be that big ass building that just became available about a month ago."

"Yeah, that's the one. The guy wanted to rent it out, but I convinced him to sell it to me, so now, it belongs to my baby," I replied.

"That's wassup, sis. I'm happy for you. And Liam, thanks for stepping up and taking care of my sister."

"No thanks needed. She deserves it and so much more, but thanks for making sure my sister is good. I couldn't have asked for a better brother-in-law than you," I told Kendrick honestly.

I liked Kendrick a lot. Of course, I wasn't cool with what he did for a living, but he always made sure my sister was straight. The way Kendrick carried himself you wouldn't even know that he was in the streets.

Soon, after we got our food, we all ate and bullshitted around.

"Before we go, I have an announcement that I want to make. I was going to wait until after the wedding, but I might as well tell y'all now. Ya boy is finally a legit businessman. I just invested in some real estate, and I left the game alone," Kendrick announced.

Lacey's face lit up with happiness, but you could also tell that she was shocked at his announcement. Today was a great day for everyone. Moments later, we all left the restaurant and headed home. When me and Kendra got home, we made love into the wee hours of the night.

Kendrick

"A'ight, babe, I have to go. The guys are waiting for me, and if you keep trying to seduce me with these sex tactics, I'm going to miss my bachelor's party, and you, my love, are going to miss your bachelorette's party."

"That's because I'd rather skip hanging out with a bunch of chicks and just stay in and do lots of freaky things to you," she said seductively, making my manhood rise to the occasion. I didn't want to bail on the fellas, but the way Lacey was looking and talking right now had a nigga about to stay in with the future Mrs.

"Lacey, you keep talking like that, and you might find yourself tied and fucked all night. Because if I pull my dick out, we ain't doing no quickies. We will both be in for the night. So what are you trying to do?" I warned, walking up in her personal space. I had to let her know that I had a little game too. Her breathing got caught in her throat, and suddenly, she wasn't feeling as freaky.

"As good as that sounds, your sister would kill me if I bailed on them. But I'm free to be tied up and fucked all night when you get back."

"So am I, so it's a date, and make sure you don't try to use that baby bump as an excuse. You're going in every position that I can think of," I told her, kissing her lips before I headed out.

Tonight, was my bachelor's party. Me, Liam, and Troy were hitting the strip joint over in Philly. I couldn't believe that I was getting married in just one week. I couldn't wait to see my baby walk down the aisle in her dress. We were having a small wedding only with the people who mattered the most. Then we would throw a bigger wedding in five years.

The doctor permitted Lacey to fly, so for our honeymoon, we were going to Hawaii. Of course, it was a surprise to where we were going. I loved surprising my baby. Lacey was just about six months, and the baby was due June 15th.

I wasn't driving over to Philly, so I went to Troy's house, and he drove.

"Nigga, I can't believe you gave up the game and all the pussy you could ever want just to bang the same chick every night," Troy said out of nowhere.

"Well, believe it. Pussy is easy to get. Besides, I have had enough pussy to last me a lifetime. Not to mention, Lacey is giving me so much more than pussy. Why just settle for pussy from random chicks when you can have love, trust, loyalty, fun, build each other up, have a family, and still get pussy all from one person? Lacey is all I need, and the only woman I want. If she wasn't, then I wouldn't be marrying her. You're gonna get lonely one day, Troy, and sex is going to be overrated until you find the right one."

"I hear you, man, but I ain't there yet."

I didn't say anything else because that was on him and his dick.

The club was everything because we had a private room, and although there were strippers here, we were kinda chilling amongst ourselves, popping bottles and talking shit about the wedding. Well, at least that's what me and Liam were doing. Troy, on the other hand, had dipped to a private room for a private session, but I wasn't beat. It wasn't any bitch in here worth catching Covid. Although, the woman that was dancing for us had to be tested ahead of time, so I guess he would be good.

A few hours later, I was heading back home to my baby. She texted me and said they were still out, so I decided to beat her home and set up the room. They didn't do much but go to dinner and then over to Kendra's house to see a stripper. It's not like Lacey could drink.

When Lacey walked into the house, I had "Meeting in My Bedroom" by Silk blasting through the speakers. I had rose petals on the floor from the front door to the bedroom. I was already as naked as the day I was born. Lacey stood in the doorway looking surprised.

"Oh my God, baby, this is so sweet," she said, covering her mouth.

"Anything for you, but no more talking from this moment forth. The only thing you can do is nod and moan, am I clear?" I asked in a stern tone. She nodded in agreement. "Now take your clothes off, walk over to the bed, lay down, then take your fingers and start pleasing yourself."

Lacey did exactly what I told her to do. I couldn't take another minute. Her moans were turning me on something serious, so I climbed on the bed and dove head-first into her wetness. After hours and hours of exploring each other's body, we finally managed to fall asleep.

*****

When I woke up the next day, it was two o'clock in the afternoon, and Lacey was still asleep. I got up to use the bathroom and handle my hygiene. When I walked back into the room, Lacey was awake.

"Good morning, baby," she said.

"You mean, good afternoon, baby. It's two PM."

"Oh my God, I didn't realize I was asleep that long."

"I know, but I guess that would be expected after the night that we had. Now we have to get ready for this dinner with everyone that's in the wedding and our parents."

"I can't wait to eat because I'm starving, and my body is weak and sore."

"I'm hungry too. But we might as well get showered so we can get going."

After our shower, we got dressed. I looked over at Lacey, and she was wearing a black body-con dress that hugged her baby bump. For six months, Lacey still didn't have a big belly, and she still looked good as shit. Just looking at her you would think she was about three or four months. At first, we were concerned, but the doctor said everything was fine and not to worry. I watched Lacey do her hair, and no matter what, I just couldn't get enough of her. I just prayed that this feeling never left.

Lacey

Today was my wedding day, and for some reason, all I've been doing is crying all day. Today was the happiest day of my life thus far, yet I was so nervous. I wasn't sure why I was so nervous. I knew that I wanted to marry this man. Plus, I was having a small wedding with people that I'm around all the time.

"Lacey, baby."

I turned around at the sound of the voice, and it was my mom. I had to admit that my mother looked beautiful. Don't get me wrong, my mom was a nice-looking woman, but on most days, she didn't do much with her appearance.

However, ever since my parents went to rehab, they have been looking better than ever. I couldn't have been more proud of them for going to rehab.

"Hey, Mom. You look beautiful."

"Thanks, baby. You look gorgeous, yourself. I can't wait to see you in your dress. How are you feeling?"

"I'm nervous, and I'm scared, and I don't know why. I've been crying all day," I told her.

"Everything that you are feeling is normal, baby, but everything is going to be just fine. You've been in love with that boy since you were thirteen years old, and don't think I don't know your little secret," she said with a sly smile.

I wasn't sure what she was talking about. "Mom, what secret?"

"I know that Kendrick took your virginity on your eighteenth birthday."

I threw my hands over my mouth in disbelief. I had no idea how she found that out. No one knew about that, or so I thought, except me and Kendrick.

"Oh my God, Mom, how did you know that?" I mean, I never told a soul. Not even Kendra.

"I know that I was always drunk, and I wish now that I wasn't, but that's in the past now. But I always paid attention to you and Liam, and I knew that y'all were going to make me proud. I love you, Lacey. You and your brother mean everything to me. And I'm sorry that it took for you to become a mother and wife for me to get my shit together."

The two of us hugged and cried. I guess that crying was something that I wasn't going to get away from tonight. After the two of us were finished crying, she handed me a beautiful pair of royal blue earrings.

"Mom, these are beautiful."

"I wore these when I married your dad, and now, I'm passing them on to you, and you can pass them on to your daughter."

After my mom left out, I thought back to my eighteenth birthday.

I was at Kendra's house. She had thrown me a little party. When it was time for me to go home, I didn't have anyone to take me because Kendra was drunk. I had one drink, and that was my first time drinking, so it hit me pretty hard. I couldn't call my parents because they were somewhere drunk themselves, and I didn't want to call Liam, so Kendrick said that he would take me. Me and Kendrick got into his car, and he pulled off. He reached over and turned the radio down. For some reason, I was nervous to be alone with him, at first.

"Happy birthday, Lacey."

"Thank you."

"So I see you're not a drinker, and my sister drinks a little too much."

We both started laughing.

"Nah, tonight was my first time. I'm a little buzzed, but I'm nothing like Kendra. I think that she had more fun at my party than I did."

"Yeah, Kendra's pretty wild. I don't know why she couldn't just be like you," he said.

I looked up at him, and the look in his eyes was intense. I sat there trying to form the right words to say to him that didn't make me sound crazy. But I needed to let him know how I felt. I wasn't sure if I would be alone with him again.

"Kendrick, I need to tell you something."

"Wassup, love?"

"I'm in love with you and have been since I was thirteen," I told him.

"In love, huh? Lacey, I'm not going to hold you. I'm digging you too. I won't say that I'm in love, but I'm feeling you too. But I don't want to take it there with you right now—"

"Why, because I'm you're little sister's best friend?" I asked cutting him off.

"Nah, because you're a good girl that deserves a good guy. I'm in these streets, and I ain't leaving no time soon. Plus, I love women and sex. I'm too young to settle down right now, so I don't want to go there with you because I like you too much to hurt you," he stated.

I had mixed feelings after his comment. "I respect your honesty, but why didn't you ever tell me that you liked me?"

"For what? I didn't want to get your hopes up. I always knew that when I was ready to settle down, I would come to find you and shoot my shot with you. And If you were still feeling me, then I would have made you mine."

I don't know what came over me, but I leaned over and kissed his lips. I thought he was going to pull back, but instead, he kissed me back. The kiss got pretty intense, pretty quick. He was the first guy I ever kissed, so I wasn't sure if I was doing it right. He finally broke the kiss and just stared at me.

"Damn, Lacey. I think you should go in the house."

"Kendrick, I want to have sex with you."

His eyes got wide, and he swallowed the lump that was in his throat. "I don't think that's a good idea. Have you been with a guy before?"

"No, I haven't. I'm saving myself for you."

"Lacey, I don't want to hurt you, so I'm going to pass. Give your virginity to someone who deserves it."

"Look, Kendrick, I don't want no one but you. I know we're not going to be together, and I'm cool with that. But I think I'm old enough to know who I want to be my first. I say we just do it and never talk about it again. I want

to give it to the man I love, and that's you. You already said that you wanted to be with me when you were ready to settle down, which means we would have sex eventually."

"You're making this hard, Lacey, but fuck it let's go," he said, backing up from the driveway in front of my house.

"Wait, where are we going?"

"To a hotel. If we're going to do this, we're going to do it right."

When we got to the hotel, we didn't waste any time getting it in. Kendrick made me feel like a woman. He did everything to my body that could be done.

Most importantly, Kendrick made sure that I was comfortable and that my first time was special. To this very day, Kendrick has been the only man that I've been with sexually. I've dated other guys, but my body strictly was for Kendrick.

"Lacey, are you okay? You look like you're daydreaming," Kendra said, interrupting me from my thoughts.

"Yeah, I'm fine. I was just thinking."

"Well, let's get you in this dress. It's time for the wedding to start."

I put on my dress, and Kendra fixed my makeup. My mom helped with the train of my dress. I looked in the mirror and couldn't believe that I was about to be someone's wife in a couple of minutes.

"Wow, princess, you look beautiful," my dad said, walking into the room.

"Thanks, Daddy."

Everyone got in a position to walk out. First, my mom and mother-in-law walked out, then Kendrick's little cousin, who was our flower girl. It was now my turn. I put my arms inside of my dad's arm and proceeded to walk down to the song.

"It feels like a lifetime, a thousand days have passed

by

since I held you, close to me

if I could see that smile from my friend

I know that I can live again,

I need you, here with me

Heaven knows what to say

even though for right now you're so far away

I hope and I pray somewhere in your heart I'll

always stay

Girl, lately my sun doesn't shine without you

Never noticed what it feels like to be without you

Feels like I took my last step and my last breath in

My life ending

Had to say just what I was feeling, girl

Cause my sun doesn't shine, sun doesn't without

you

This is more for me than for you

Girl, I finally see there's no substitute

For what we have

Do you know how much I love you

And what we share

I can't forget, Girl a love like yours

I'll never let just slip away, just promise that you'll

stay

Heaven knows what to say

Even though for right now you're so far away

Gonna tell you and show you

Do whatever I can do to get back to you

Girl lately my sun doesn't shine without you

Never noticed what it feels like to be without you

Feels like I took my last and my last breath in

My life ending

Had to just what I feeling, girl

Cause my sun doesn't shine, sun doesn't shine

without you..."

When I got up to the altar, my face was already soaked with tears. The music stopped playing, and I stood there looking at the tears running down Kendrick's face. They made me cry even harder.

"Who giveth this woman away?" the Pastor asked.

"I do," my father answered, handing me over to Kendrick.

Kendrick looked at me like I was the greatest thing in the world.

"Lacey, you're the most beautiful woman I've ever seen in my life," he said, placing a kiss on my lips. The both of us were still crying. I knew I would be emotional, but I wasn't expecting all this.

"I see you ready to jump straight to the end of the ceremony," the Pastor said, causing everyone to laugh.

"I'm sorry, Pastor. I couldn't help it. Do you see how beautiful she looks?"

The two of us exchanged our vows and rings before the Pastor said the twelve magical words that made our marriage official.

"I now pronounce you husband and wife. You may kiss your bride."

Kendrick and I kissed like we were the only two in the room. Everyone was clapping and cheering. We finally broke the kiss and walked out holding hands. After the pictures, it was time for the reception, but I was ready for the honeymoon. It was now time to walk into the reception hall.

"Introducing, for the first time, Mr. and Mrs. Kendrick Mason!"

Everyone clapped as we walked in, and I couldn't have been happier or proud to be Mrs. Kendrick Mason.

Kendrick

My life couldn't be any better right now. Lacey and I have been married for six months now, and it still feels like it was just yesterday since we got married. I know that they say that no marriage was perfect, but I had to disagree. I was in love with being married to Lacey. Besides my wedding day, the next happiest moment in my life was watching my daughter make her way into this world. We named our princess Kimora Lynn Mason. She was so beautiful. With my light complexion and Lacey's chocolate complexion, Kimora was a perfect, brown-skinned complexion.

I was in the house with my daughter while Lacey went to her shop so she could check-in and do inventory. Her shop was doing great, and she was about to open up another one in a few months closer to where we lived. I surprised Lacey with the dream home that she told me she'd wanted when we first started dating. I started having our house built a few years ago so I could surprise her with it once we were married. I'd always been hopeful that she would one day be my wife. So when we got back from our honeymoon, instead of driving to my house or her apartment, I drove her to our new home. She was surprised and excited, and I loved putting a smile on my wife's face.

As far as myself, I was just enjoying being a happily married man. I was focused on my real estate business as well. I opened up a real estate company, and I bought some real estate to rent out. So shit was all good with me. Lacey loved Hawaii so much that we bought a vacation home there. We're having a couple's getaway for two weeks for Kendra's birthday at the end of the month. It's supposed to be Kendra, Liam, Troy, and his girlfriend, Tisha. Yup, y'all heard right. Troy has finally made someone his girlfriend.

Speaking of relationships, Kendra has no idea that Liam is going to propose to her in Hawaii. My sister has come a long way, and I couldn't have been more proud of her. Kendra opened up her boutique and named it Kendra's fashion boutique. Not only does she own a boutique, but she just started designing clothes for a few models. As far as Liam, my bro was doing his thing. He just opened up another bike shop over in Philly, so everything was good on our end. Love trumps all, and sometimes, it just takes the right woman or man to elevate you to the highest levels and make you wanna be a better you.

THE END